The Night Before Christmas

BY

Clement C. Moore

ILLUSTRATED BY

Lynn Ferris

ARIEL BOOKS

ANDREWS AND McMEEL

KANSAS CITY

Library of Congress Cataloging-in-Publication Data

Moore, Clement Clarke, 1779–1863.
    The night before Christmas / by Clement C. Moore ; illustrated by
  Lynn Ferris.
        p.   cm.
      "Ariel Books."
      Summary: The well-known poem about an important Christmas Eve
  visitor.
      ISBN 0–8362–4917–8 : $6.95
      1. Santa Claus—Juvenile poetry. 2. Christmas—Juvenile poetry.
  3. Children's poetry, American. [1. Santa Claus—Poetry. 2. Christmas—
  Poetry. 3. American poetry. 4. Narrative poetry.] I. Ferris, Lynn
  Bywaters,   ill. II. Title.
  PS2429.M5N5   1991c
  811'.2—dc20   91–14211
                                                                          CIP
First Printing, September 1991   AC
Third Printing, September 1992

Design: Susan Hood and Mike Hortens
Art Direction: Armand Eisen, Mike Hortens, and Julie Phillips
Art Production: Lynn Wine
Production: Julie Miller and Lisa Shadid

The Night
Before Christmas

'Twas the night before Christmas, when all
    through the house
Not a creature was stirring, not even a mouse.

*The stockings were hung by the chimney with
 care,
In hopes that St. Nicholas soon would be there.
The children were nestled all snug in their beds,
While visions of sugarplums danced in their
 heads;*

And Mama in her kerchief, and I in my cap,
Had just settled our brains for a long winter's
    nap,
When out on the lawn there arose such a clatter,
I sprang from my bed to see what was the
    matter.
Away to the window I flew like a flash,
Tore open the shutters and threw up the sash.
The moon on the breast of the new-fallen snow
Gave a luster of midday to objects below;

When what to my wondering eyes should appear
But a miniature sleigh and eight tiny reindeer,
With a little old driver, so lively and quick,
I knew in a moment it must be St. Nick!

More rapid than eagles his coursers they came,
And he whistled and shouted and called them by
    name:
"Now, Dasher! Now, Dancer! Now, Prancer
    and Vixen!
On, Comet! On, Cupid! On, Donder and
    Blitzen!
To the top of the porch! To the top of the wall!
Now dash away! Dash away! Dash away, all!"

As dry leaves that before the wild hurricane fly,
When they meet with an obstacle, mount to the
   sky,
So up to the housetop the coursers they flew,
With a sleigh full of toys—and St. Nicholas too.
And then, in a twinkling, I heard on the roof
The prancing and pawing of each little hoof.
As I drew in my head and was turning around,
Down the chimney St. Nicholas came with a
   bound.

He was dressed all in fur, from his head to his
    foot,
And his clothes were all tarnished with ashes
    and soot;
A bundle of toys he had flung on his back,
And he looked like a peddler just opening his
    pack.
His eyes, how they twinkled! His dimples, how
    merry!
His cheeks were like roses, his nose like a cherry!
His droll little mouth was drawn up like a bow,
And the beard on his chin was as white as the
    snow.
The stump of a pipe he held tight in his teeth,
And the smoke, it encircled his head like a
    wreath.

He had a broad face and a little round belly
That shook, when he laughed, like a bowl full of
    jelly.
He was chubby and plump, a right jolly old elf,
And I laughed when I saw him, in spite of
    myself.
A wink of his eye and a twist of his head
Soon gave me to know I had nothing to dread.

*He spoke not a word, but went straight to his
  work,*
*And filled all the stockings, then turned with a
  jerk,*
And laying a finger aside of his nose,
And giving a nod, up the chimney he rose.

He sprang to his sleigh, to his team gave a
   whistle,
And away they all flew like the down of a
   thistle.
But I heard him exclaim, ere he drove out of
   sight,
"Happy Christmas to all, and to all a good
   night!"